TRUCKS GALORE

Peter Stein
illustrated by Bob Staake

WALKER BOOKS
AND SUBSIDIARIES
LONDON · BOSTON · SYDNEY · AUCKLAND

Wide truck, thin truck,
out truck, in truck.
Hot truck, cold truck,
big bad BOLD truck!

Strong truck, weak truck,
hide-and-seek truck.
Rock truck, dirt truck,
Yum – DESSERT truck!

Trucks and MORE trucks!
Open-door trucks!
Heavy-load trucks!
Shake-the-road trucks!

Baaa truck. Moo truck.
Cock-a-doodle-DOO truck.
Oink truck. Cluck truck.
Quackin' in a duck truck!

Trucks constructing,
working hard.
Trucks protecting,
standing guard.

Hey, you trucks!
CLEAN UP THAT YARD!

Outer-space truck.
Out-of-place truck.
Song-and-dance truck.
Lost-his-pants truck!

Burning building!
Screeching tyres!
Water gushing!
Trucks for FIRES!

Bird truck, weird truck,
bushy-beard truck.
Round truck, bent truck,
circus-tent truck!

Trucks and trucks and
even MORE trucks!
Loaded roads of
trucks GALORE trucks!

HOT DOG TOWN

Stranded auto,
stuck in muck.
Not for long ...
TOW IT, TRUCK!

Stinky RUBBISH ...
outta here!
Trucks can make it
DISAPPEAR!

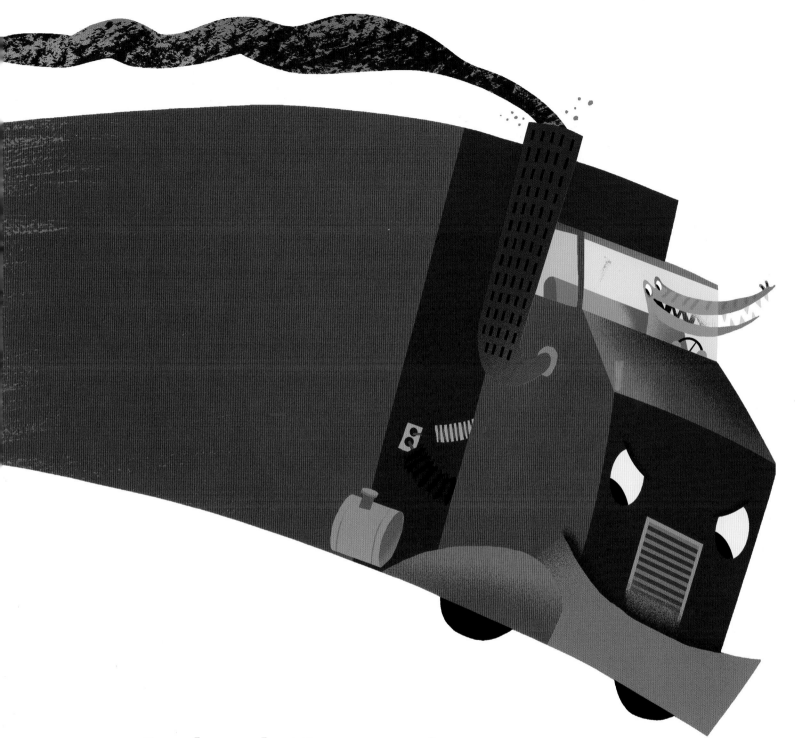

High-tech NEW truck —
go, go, GO!
Creaky OLD truck
go ... so ... slow.

Silly SMASH trucks!
Crazy CRASH trucks!
Lunging LEAP trucks!
Time for sleep, trucks.

A SEA-LIFE truck –
what fishy fun!
Look out below –
you might CATCH one!

FRESH
FISH

Trucks with cakes
and big balloons!
Party trucks play
party tunes!

Daring brave truck!
In-a-cave truck!
Creaky-bridge truck.
On-a-ridge truck.

Trucks bring presents –
you're in luck!
Pull the handle ...
THANK YOU, TRUCK!

Trucks will work
till work is done.
Trucks are COOL —
they're number one!

A truck
for YOU?
Hey, sounds
like FUN!

For Gabriel and Elias –
my backseat drivers who moved up front
P. S.

To Oscar Glenn March, inventor of the mud flap
B. S.

First published 2017 by Walker Books Ltd
87 Vauxhall Walk, London SE11 5HJ

2 4 6 8 10 9 7 5 3 1

Text © 2017 Peter Stein
Illustrations © 2017 Bob Staake

This book has been typeset in Zalderdash

Printed in China

British Library Cataloguing in Publication Data:
a catalogue record for this book is available from the British Library

ISBN 978-1-4063-8049-1

www.walker.co.uk